Did You Carry the Flag Today, Charley?

YEARLING BOOKS/YOUNG YEARLINGS/YEARLING CLASSICS are designed especially to entertain and enlighten young people. Patricia Reilly Giff, consultant to this series, received her bachelor's degree from Marymount College and a master's degree in history from St. John's University. She holds a Professional Diploma in Reading and a Doctorate of Humane Letters from Hofstra University. She was a teacher and reading consultant for many years, and is the author of numerous books for young readers.

For a complete listing of all Yearling titles, write to
Dell Readers Service,
P.O. Box 1045,
South Holland, IL 60473.

Did You Carry the Flag Today, Charley?

by Rebecca Caudill

Illustrated by Nancy Grossman

A Yearling Book

Published by
Bantam Doubleday Dell Books for Young Readers
a division of
Bantam Doubleday Dell Publishing Group, Inc.
1540 Broadway
New York, New York 10036

ISBN: 0-440-40092-9

Reprinted by arrangement with Henry Holt and Company,
Inc.

Printed in the United States of America

June 1988

13   12   11   10   9   8   7   6

OPM

For Mildred
through whose eyes as well as
through my own I observed a
Little School

Did You Carry the Flag Today, Charley?

1

To get to Charley Cornett's house, you turn left off the highway at Main Street, drive to the edge of town, and cross a bridge. There you take another left turn, and you are on your way. You can't get lost because there is only one road to follow. It is a blacktop. It looks like a black ribbon tied around the mountain, sometimes high on the mountainside, sometimes low in the narrow creek bottom.

11

When you have gone twenty miles or so, you will come to Charley's house. You will miss it unless you keep a sharp lookout. The roof of the house and the chimney are all you can see, for the road at that point is high on the mountainside, and Charley's house is down the mountain below the road.

It isn't a big house. In it live Charley, his mother and his father, his four brothers, Claude, Jim, Jack, and John, and his five sisters, Connie, Amy, Dottie, Mary, and Betsy.

Charley was hunting for crawdads beside the creek that ran below his house when he heard a putt-putting sound coming along the blacktop. He left off hunting for crawdads, looked up, and watched the road. Rounding a sharp curve jounced a jeep. Miss Amburgey, Charley guessed. Miss Amburgey taught at the Raccoon Hollow School and she drove a jeep.

As Charley watched, the jeep pulled off the road and stopped in front of his house. He raced up the hill to the house, climbed the steep steps to the back door, and hurried through the kitchen to the living room. There, in the best rocking chair, sat Miss Amburgey, talking with Charley's mother.

"Hello, Charley," said Miss Amburgey as he en-

tered the room. Her face was smiley and friendly.

"I came to see you and your mother about your coming to Little School this summer. We're having Little School for four- and five-year-olds at Raccoon Hollow for six weeks. How old are you?"

Charley crowded into the chair beside his mother. He grinned broadly at Miss Amburgey.

"Four a goin' on five," he told her.

"He'll be five next week," Mrs. Cornett said. "He looks mighty little to be five. But of course you can't always judge a boy by his size. Charley's made little. But I warn you now. He's plumb full of curiosity. He's got to find out about things."

"We like boys with curiosity," Miss Amburgey said. "I believe you'd like Little School, Charley. And I'm sure we'd enjoy having you."

"Yes'm," said Charley, grinning more broadly and showing that his two front upper teeth were missing.

"What happened to your teeth?" asked Miss Amburgey.

"Curiosity," answered Mrs. Cornett. "He just had to find out how an apple is fastened on to a limb. So he climbed an apple tree and crawled out too far on

14

the limb. Down came Charley on his face, and out came his teeth."

"Well, we'll have lots of things for you to find out about at Little School, Charley," Miss Amburgey told him. "I'll tell Mr. Mullins to pick you up on the bus Monday morning. Be waiting for him in front of your house."

Monday morning when the July sun soared up over the mountain peaks and began heating up the hollow, and the cicadas started their shrill fiddling, Charley, barefoot, scrubbed, and wearing a clean shirt and faded jeans, climbed the steep path from his house up to the blacktop. There he waited beside the mailbox.

"Charley, it'll be an hour before that bus comes," his mother called to him from the doorway.

Charley did not answer. He looked up at the Appalachian mountain peaks towering all around him, gauzy green in the heat, splashed with the dark green of pines. He remembered the day he and Uncle Hawk had climbed to the tiptop of the fire tower on Pilot Knob where they could see mountain peaks going on and on, and the sky, like an upturned bowl, rimming them in.

15

Down the notch between every two peaks, Uncle Hawk told Charley, ran a trickle of water. There must be a thousand licks and branches and creeks, Uncle Hawk reckoned, and every one of them had a name, just as every boy had a name. Grapevine and Cottonpatch. Wild Dog and Wolf. Sugar and Salt. Cutshin and Betty Troublesome and Granny Dismal.

One day, thought Charley, he'd climb to the top of one of those peaks and find where the trickle of water started.

"Ain't you getting tired standing there?" his mother called.

Charley did not answer. He wondered instead about Uncle Hawk. For years Uncle Hawk had worked at the Benham coal mines. Six weeks before he'd been laid off. He'd been laid off too many times, Uncle Hawk said. He was through with coal mining. He was going out into the world, far beyond the rim of the mountains, to some big city and find himself another job. Where was Uncle Hawk now? Charley wondered. What kind of job had he found? What was a big city like?

When it was almost time for the bus, Mrs. Cornett

climbed the path to the blacktop and waited beside Charley. One by one Charley's brothers and sisters also climbed the path.

Charley's father hobbled to the door on his crutches. His back had been hurt in a coal mine. He couldn't climb the steep path very well.

"Be a good boy, Charley," he called.

"You be sure to answer when Miss Amburgey calls you, Charley," his mother cautioned him. "You don't always answer when I call you."

"There'll be four or five people calling you at Little School," John told him.

"Four or five? Besides Miss Amburgey?" asked Charley.

"Sure. There's Mr. Sizemore and Mr. Webb, and Miss Sturgill and Mr. Champion. Mr. Champion, he's the principal. If he calls, you better say, 'Yes, Sir,' and say it polite like, and get a move on—in Mr. Champion's direction."

Charley grinned. "I ain't scared of any of them," he said.

"You don't say 'ain't' in Little School," Claude told him. "You have to talk proper."

"When the bell rings," said Amy, "you quit quick

whatever you're doing, and get in line."

"When you've finished your lunch," said Dottie, "you carry your dishes to the kitchen without being told."

"And don't lick the top of the salt shaker," cautioned Connie. "You'll catch it from the teacher at the table if you do."

"Children," Mrs. Cornett scolded, "you make it sound like Charley's going off to jail. Can't you think of something nice about Little School to tell him?"

"Oh, there's things at school, Charley, like you've never seen before," said Jim. "All sort of things to play with—balls, and puzzles to put together, and games."

"And there's a library with shelves crammed with books," said Betsy, "and Miss Sturgill lets you look at 'em."

"I don't like books," said Charley.

"How do you know you don't like books when you never had one?" asked Betsy. "Miss Sturgill tells you stories, too."

"In Mr. Sizemore's room, you can paint pictures and color with crayons, and make things out of clay—every color of clay, Charley," Jack told him. "It isn't like making things out of mud."

"At school, Charley, you don't wash your hands in a washpan," explained Mary. "There's a big white bowl fastened to the wall in every room. You turn a knob in the middle of it, and out squirts water into the bowl. That's where you wash your hands."

"Aw!" Charley grinned. " I don't believe that. Water squirting out of the wall!"

"Wait and see!" said Mary.

"At the end of every school day, Charley," said Claude, "Miss Amburgey chooses some boy or girl who has been specially good that day to carry a flag and march at the head of the line to the bus."

Charley grinned. "I bet I carry it today."

"Yeah, I bet," said Jack. "First thing we're going to ask when you get home is, 'Did you carry the flag today, Charley?'"

"Here she comes!" called Mr. Cornett from the doorway.

Everybody grew quiet. Behind a spur of the mountain, they heard the bus droning along the blacktop.

At the mailbox, the bus rolled to a stop.

"All aboard for Little School, Charley!" Mr.

Mullins, the driver, called out as he swung the door wide.

"Bye, Charley!" called the brothers and sisters. Mr. Cornett waved from the doorway. Mrs. Cornett put a hand on Charley's shoulder.

"Be a good boy, Charley," she said to him. "And I'm counting on it; you'll like Little School."

Charley looked around the bus as he entered. It seemed crammed with boys and girls.

"Right back there you'll find a seat, Charley," said Mr. Mullins.

The door swung shut and down the blacktop rolled the bus. All the Cornetts stood looking after it.

"Do you think Charley will get to carry the flag?" asked Betsy. "On his very first day of school?"

"No," said Claude and Jack, and Amy and Mary together.

"We'll know when he gets home tonight," said Mrs. Cornett.

2

Mr. Mullins stopped the bus beside the playground and opened the door. Out tumbled the children. Some hurried. Some trudged along with their eyes on the ground and their thumbs in their mouths. Charley pushed his way among them to be the first on the playground.

Miss Amburgey waited for them at the playground gate.

"Good morning, boys and girls," she said. "You have fifteen minutes to play before we go indoors. Mr. Webb and Mr. Sizemore are here to play with you. When I ring the bell, come here to the gate."

Through the gate ran Charley. He wanted to see all the things his brothers and sisters had told him about. Sure enough, there were the balls, lying beside the wire fence—big ones and little ones, hard ones and soft ones. A man stood near them.

"Hello!" said the man. "I'm Mr. Webb. You must be Charley Cornett."

Charley grinned. "How'd you know my name?"

"I know more than your name," said Mr. Webb. "I know how old you are, and where you live, and how you knocked out your teeth."

Charley's grin broadened. "How'd you know all that now?"

"It's part of my job to know all that," explained Mr. Webb.

He picked up a ball from beside the fence. "How would you like to play catch with some of the other boys?" He threw the ball to Charley.

Charley shook his head. "Could I see what else is here?" he asked.

"All right," agreed Mr. Webb. "Look around. See you later."

Charley discovered his brothers and sisters hadn't told him half the things that were on the playground. There were swings and a slide. There were teeters and a sand pile. There was a rope to jump. Charley tried them all. But what looked like the most fun was one thick plank laid on the ground and another laid across the middle of it. A girl stood on each end of the top plank. First one girl jumped, and her end of the plank flew up. When she came down on it, hard, the other end flew up and the other girl bounced high in the air. Up and down. Up and down. Harder and harder and higher.

"Let me do that," said Charley.

Just then the bell rang. As the girls jumped off the plank and started running to the gate, Charley squatted on the ground to see what made the plank bounce.

"Charley!" he heard Miss Amburgey calling.

He didn't answer. He hadn't yet found what he was looking for.

"Charley Cornett!"

This time Miss Amburgey's voice had a certain

sound in it. Charley joined the other boys and girls. Miss Amburgey laid her hand on his shoulder.

"Boys and girls," said Miss Amburgey, "you are to be divided into four groups. Each morning one group will go first with Mr. Sizemore, one with Mr. Webb, one with Miss Sturgill, and one with me. During the day you will go to different rooms, be with different teachers, and do different things. Listen carefully as I read your names," she added, "and go quietly with your teacher."

Charley hoped Miss Amburgey would send him with Mr. Sizemore. Mr. Sizemore's room, he remembered, was where the clay and crayons were. But Miss Amburgey didn't send him with Mr. Sizemore.

Well, thought Charley, he'd like to go with Mr. Webb. He liked Mr. Webb, and Mr. Webb knew all about him. But Miss Amburgey didn't send him with Mr. Webb.

Miss Sturgill? It would be something to see shelves all over a room and all crammed with books. And he might like to hear a story. But Miss Amburgey didn't send him with Miss Sturgill.

Miss Amburgey called his name in her group.

At once the four groups started walking quietly toward the schoolhouse.

That is, they all walked but Charley. He ran.

As he ran past Miss Amburgey, she caught him by the hand. "Remember, Charley, you walk with your own group," she said.

Charley hated having his hand held like a baby.

Once inside Miss Amburgey's schoolroom, Charley looked around. Little chairs stood in a circle, with one big chair among them. Behind the big chair was a blackboard, and in a trough underneath lay pieces of chalk. Low tables stood at one side of the room. And there—there, fastened to the wall, was the white washbowl! And there in the middle of it was the knob that you turned to let the water squirt out of the wall.

Charley hurried over to the bowl, turned the knob just a little, and out of the wall through a short spout came a trickle of water. He turned the knob a little more, and out of the wall poured a stream of water.

With both hands he turned the knob as far as it would go. Out of the wall water came gushing.

"Charley!" he heard Miss Amburgey call.

Charley turned the knob backward and watched

the stream of water grow smaller. He turned it forward again and watched the stream grow larger.

Suddenly Miss Amburgey's hand closed over his hands and turned the knob backward all the way. Then Miss Amburgey led Charley to the little chair next to the big chair.

"This will be your chair, Charley," she explained as she sat down in the big chair beside him. "You will sit in it every morning. See if you can sit as quietly as the other boys and girls."

Charley sat down and grew quiet.

"First, let's all get acquainted," said Miss Amburgey. "Let's each of us tell our own names, so that everyone else will know them. That way we can make friends. All of you know my name—Miss Amburgey. Now, beginning with Charley, let's go around the circle. Charley?"

"Charley Cornett," answered Charley loud and clear.

"Good!" said Miss Amburgey. "I hope all of you will speak out the way Charley did so that the rest of us can hear."

Around the circle the children named themselves. Then each child tried naming all the others.

When they had finished, they sang songs: "Go Tell Aunt Rhody" and "Coming Round the Mountain." Then for a while they put together puzzles— Jack and Jill, Little Miss Muffett, Old King Cole, Little Boy Blue, and many others.

In the middle of the morning Miss Amburgey said, "Boys and girls, milk and cookies will be brought to the room for you every morning. They will be here soon. You may put your puzzles in order in their boxes now, and stack them in the cabinet neatly. Then wash your hands. We never eat without washing our hands, do we?"

"Do we get to wash 'em in that big white bowl over there?" asked Charley.

"Yes," said Miss Amburgey.

There was a shoving of chairs and a shuffling of feet as the boys and girls hurried to put the puzzles away.

"You may form a line now to wash your hands," said Miss Amburgey. "Bessie, would you like to lead the line?"

Miss Amburgey herself went ahead of the children to the washbowl, turned the knob, and let a little stream of water flow out of the spout.

"We always use soap when we wash our hands," Miss Amburgey told the children.

"Where's the soap?" asked Charley.

"In the soap dish," said Miss Amburgey, "right here above the washbowl."

Charley stared at the soap. "Blue soap! I never heard tell of blue soap," he said.

"How would you like to stand here beside the washbowl, Charley," asked Miss Amburgey, "and as each child finishes washing his hands hand him a towel? We all use separate towels and put them in the wastebasket when we dry our hands."

"Yes'm, Miss Amburgey," said Charley. He hurried to stand by the washbowl. "You mean—does every single one get a towel? And then throw it in the wastebasket?"

"These are paper towels, Charley," explained Miss Amburgey, "so that each of you may have your own towel."

"Paper towels!" muttered Charley. "Paper towels and blue soap!"

As the children moved along in line, Charley handed each one a towel. He figured out that he would be the last to use the soap and the washbowl.

He liked that because nobody would be hurrying him from behind.

At last the other children finished, and sat down at the tables to wait for their milk and cookies. Charley laid his towel on the window sill beside the washbowl and took the blue soap from the dish. In his hands, the soap felt slippery, like a fish just out of water. He turned it in his hands and looked at both sides of it. He held it to his nose and sniffed. It smelled! It smelled like an apple tree full of blossoms!

He put his hands in the stream of water, and rolled and rolled the soap in them. He put the soap in the dish, and looked at his hands. He decided they weren't soapy enough yet. Again he took the soap and rolled it in his hands, over and over.

From the corner of his eye he saw Miss Amburgey watching.

He sniffed the soap once more, laid it in the dish, and gave the knob a turn. As he held his soapy hands under the gushing water, he heard Miss Amburgey coming toward him.

Why couldn't he stop the water by holding his hand under the spout where it came out of the wall? he wondered.

He laid one of his hands in the palm of the other, and pressed them tight against the spout.

"Charley Cornett! Look what you've done!" shouted half the boys and girls in the room.

Charley looked. Miss Amburgey had turned off the water. But there she stood with water dripping down the front of her dress. There sat the boys and girls, half of them with water running down their faces. Charley realized then that his face too was dripping water. Why, he was wet all down his front. The floor around was wet. The chairs were wet. The tables were wet. The window was splattered with water.

That evening when Charley stepped off the school bus, his mother was waiting for him. His father hobbled to the door. His brothers and sisters came running.

"Did you carry the flag today, Charley?" asked Betsy.

Charley looked at their faces and grinned. He scratched one leg with the big toe of his other foot.

"Well-l-l," he said.

"No," said the Cornetts all together. "Charley didn't carry the flag today."

3

On Tuesday and Friday afternoons Charley's group went to the library the last half hour before the bus came to take the children home.

Charley liked the library and he didn't like the library. He couldn't imagine why anybody wanted so many books standing everywhere on shelves. He felt smothered by so many shelves full of books.

But he liked the days when Miss Sturgill let them play games. He especially liked the days when she sat on a stool in a corner and told stories to the boys and girls sitting around her in small chairs.

Charley had three favorite stories. One was about a girl named Mollie Whuppie, one was about a boy named Jack who grew a beanstalk that reached to the sky, and the other was about some elves who played tricks on a shoemaker.

On Friday afternoon of the second week of Little School, clouds were gathering in the sky as Charley's group went to the library. The air was still and sultry. Not a leaf on a tree stirred. Rain threatened.

"Let's have a story today," suggested Miss Sturgill as soon as the children were gathered. "What story would you like to hear?"

"Mollie Whuppie!" shouted Charley.

Charley had learned that when Miss Sturgill's voice was rising, something exciting was going to happen in the story she was telling. That day when he heard it rising, he tilted his chair far forward. When Miss Sturgill reached an exciting part of Mollie Whuppie, he let his chair back with a loud bump.

36

Miss Sturgill seemed not to hear. She went right on with Mollie Whuppie.

When her voice began rising again, Charley once more tilted his chair forward. The children sitting near him tilted theirs forward too. When Miss Sturgill reached another exciting part, *bump* went Charley's chair. *Bump, bump, bump* went other chairs.

"Charley," said Miss Sturgill, "bring your chair up here and sit beside me."

With Miss Sturgill's hand on the back of his chair, Charley couldn't bump. But the other children could. And Charley could make faces at them. Only one or two were listening to the story. The others were giggling at Charley.

Miss Sturgill sighed. She asked, "How would you like to play 'Bring a comb and play upon it, Marching here we come'?"

The boys and girls had played that game the week before. Noisily they shoved their chairs into a corner.

"Vinnie," said Miss Sturgill, "you may go in front and play on the comb. The rest may march behind you."

Vinnie, pretending she was playing on a comb, tooted a tune and marched in and out among the bookshelves from one end of the library to the other. The other boys and girls stomped noisily behind her. Charley, at the end of the line, was behind the farthest shelf of books when Vinnie reached the storytelling corner.

As he glanced at the books, he wondered why all of them stood on the shelves with their backs turned out. He stood for a minute, looking at them. It seemed to him they ought to turn their faces toward people.

"Let's play 'Tippy Tiptoes' next," he heard Miss Sturgill say. "See how quietly you can tiptoe. Lisa Ann, you may lead this time."

Off in the storytelling corner the boys and girls began to tiptoe. They were so quiet Charley could scarcely hear them. He too was quiet as he sat on the floor, and turned the books on the bottom shelf one by one with their faces out.

As he turned the books, Charley heard rain patter on the stone walk outside the open door. Soon the patter turned into a downpour.

"Where's Charley?" asked Miss Sturgill.

"Here," said Charley, stepping out from behind the shelf.

"Were you tiptoeing back there all by yourself?" Miss Sturgill asked.

Charley grinned at her.

"Would you like to play another game now," asked Miss Sturgill of the boys and girls, "or would you like to hear another story?"

"Another game," said the boys and girls.

"Let's play 'Christopher Robin goes hoppity, hoppity,'" suggested Danny.

"All right, Danny. You may be the leader this time," said Miss Sturgill.

With Danny at the head of the line, the boys and girls began reciting the poem about Christopher Robin. As they recited, they hopped about the library, in and out among the bookshelves.

Charley, hopping near the open door, suddenly had an idea. He hopped right out into the rain. He had never hopped in rain before. He liked it. He liked it so well that he kept on hopping, right up the mountain path back of the library.

"Charley!" he heard Miss Sturgill calling from the doorway. "Come in out of the rain this minute."

Down the path hopped Charley, through the doorway. He was dripping wet.

"Charley," said Miss Sturgill in her most scolding voice, "you are not to leave this room again until the rain stops. No one is to leave until the rain stops. If it is still raining when the bus comes, it will wait for you."

Hoppity, hoppity, around and around the boys and girls continued to go. Charley joined them, leaving wet tracks on the library floor. He hopped in and out among the shelves and in corners and out of them. Then, all at once, he found himself in front of the open door again just when the rain was falling hardest. And before he knew it, out he had hopped.

Up the mountain path he hopped, and down again. At the door Miss Sturgill met him.

"Charley," she said, "you can't come in. I told you not to go out again in the rain and you heard me."

"But—but, Miss Sturgill, I'm—I'm getting mighty wet," Charley said.

"Well," said Miss Sturgill, "it's a nice warm rain and it won't hurt you. But it would hurt the library, wouldn't it, if you came in and dripped all over the

floor? So just enjoy yourself out there."

Charley stood looking at her a minute. Then slowly he walked away. He didn't feel like hopping up the mountain path again, so he walked up the mountain a way and stood under a white oak tree. There he listened to the big drops of rain patter on the leaves and watched them splash on a rock and break into little drops that bounced up in a circle.

After a while Charley left the tree and sat down in the middle of an open grassy place with no trees around to protect him from the rain. He rolled himself up like a ball with his head between his knees, and locked his arms tightly about his knees.

"Miss Sturgill," said Vinnie, looking out the window, "Charley's crying."

"Well," said Miss Sturgill, "Charley must learn to obey. And the rain isn't really hurting him."

The bus came and the rain still fell, though it was slackening. Still Charley sat rolled up like a ball where the rain could hit him hardest and make him wettest.

Then, all at once, the rain was over, the sun came out, and the bell rang for the boys and girls to go to the bus.

As Miss Sturgill was lining them up, Charley came bursting into the library.

"Miss Sturgill," he asked, "can a rock talk?"

"Stand outside, Charley, so you don't drip on the floor," Miss Sturgill told him. "I never heard a rock talk," she added.

"No," said Charley, backing out of the library, "I don't mean, can a rock talk. I mean. . ." Charley fidgeted as he tried to think of the right word. "I mean, can a rock—uh, can a rock feel?"

"Why do you ask that?" asked Miss Sturgill.

"Because I want to know," said Charley.

"That's something I never thought about, Charley," Miss Sturgill said. "I'll have to think about it and see if I can find the answer."

"You know what I was doing out there?" asked Charley.

"You were getting soaked to the skin," said Miss Sturgill. "And I don't know what your mother is going to think about your disobeying me."

"I was making out like I was a rock sitting there on the side of the hill in the rain," explained Charley. "And I was making out like I was dusty where people had stepped on me, and snakes had curled around

44

me, and lizards and spiders and ants had crawled over me, and squirrels had cracked hickory nuts on me and left the shells lying on me. And I was hot, too. And the rain fell on me and washed me off and made me feel so cool and clean. Do you reckon a rock could feel that?"

"Charley," said Miss Sturgill, "you've given me something to think about. Ask me the next time you come to the library and see if I have found the answer. Run now, so you don't miss the bus."

Down the hill ran Charley toward the bus. Andy was holding the flag, waiting for him. The other boys and girls were already inside.

"Hurry, slowpoke!" called Andy.

"Jumpin' Jehosaphat!" exclaimed Mr. Mullins as Charley stepped into the bus. "What have you been into now? Did you fall in the creek?"

"Nope," said Charley. He found an empty seat beside Jerry and started to sit down in it.

"Hey!" said Jerry, "I don't want you sitting by me, dripping like a big block of ice."

"Charley," said Mr. Mullins, "I don't believe anybody wants you sitting beside him. You come up here in front and stand where you can drip your

45

puddles. What happened to you anyway?"

"He ran out in the rain when Miss Sturgill told him not to. So he had to stay out," explained half a dozen children.

Charley held his head jauntily as he flung back at them, "But you don't know what else happened."

At the Cornetts' mailbox Mr. Mullins stopped the bus and opened the door. As Charley stepped out, his hair slick with rain, his clothes soggy with water, all the Cornetts gasped.

"No," said Connie, shaking her head. "Charley didn't carry the flag today."

4

Of all the rooms at Little School, the one Charley liked best was Mr. Sizemore's. Charley's group went there the last half hour of every Wednesday.

In Mr. Sizemore's room the children made things of clay. They colored with crayons. They painted pictures with their fingers on big sheets of paper. They built houses and fences and calf pens with blocks. One day a boy built a mountain with blocks. On the mountain top he put a little flag.

The blocks were in a small room just off Mr. Sizemore's classroom. On a low shelf in that room stood big jars of clay of many colors.

One Wednesday afternoon, Mr. Sizemore said, "Suppose we paint today."

All the boys and girls liked to paint with their fingers. Whenever they sat at the tables to paint, Mr. Sizemore placed a piece of drawing paper in front of each of them. Then he took a large jar from a shelf, and went around the room pouring a blob of starch on each piece of paper.

Charley was sitting at the end of his table. He laid both hands flat in the blob of starch and smeared, and smeared, around and around. "It feels slick, like ice," he said, and he smeared some more.

"Ready for the blue stuff, Mr. Sizemore," he called.

"Is everyone ready?" asked Mr. Sizemore.

Around the room Mr. Sizemore went from table to table, sprinkling a few drops of tempera paint on each paper. He sprinkled blue paint on some papers, red paint on some, and yellow paint on some.

"I want some of every color, Mr. Sizemore," said Charley.

Mr. Sizemore sprinkled blue and red and yellow on Charley's paper.

"You know what I'm painting?" Charley said to Vinnie who sat next to him.

"No. What?" asked Vinnie.

"A rainbow," said Charley.

"I saw a rainbow one time," said Vinnie.

"Where was it?" asked Charley.

"In the sky, of course," said Vinnie. "Where'd you think it would be?"

"I saw a rainbow on the ground one time," said Charley.

"Mr. Sizemore," said Vinnie, "you know what Charley said? He said he saw a rainbow on the ground one time. He didn't, did he?"

"I did, too," said Charley.

"Where was it, Charley?" asked Mr. Sizemore.

"In a puddle," said Charley. "At a filling station."

"You could have seen one there," said Mr. Sizemore. "In an oil puddle. It wouldn't have been exactly like the rainbow you see in the sky, but it could have had some of the same colors."

"See?" Charley said to Vinnie.

Charley smeared and smeared.

"Done, Mr. Sizemore," he called.

Mr. Sizemore wrote on one corner of Charley's paper in big black letters, CHARLEY.

"Its name is Rainbow in a Puddle at a Filling Station," said Charley.

Mr. Sizemore wrote on one edge of the paper, RAINBOW IN A PUDDLE AT A FILLING STATION. With two clothespins he fastened Charley's picture on a cord stretched along the wall. When it was dry he would put it in a big folder labeled CHARLEY with all the other pictures Charley had painted. On the last day of school, Charley could take the folder home and show his mother all his pictures.

"Now I want to make something out of clay," Charley said.

"All right," said Mr. Sizemore. "You may get some clay off the shelf."

Charley went to the block room and chose some pink clay. Back at the table he pinched off a piece of the clay and rolled it in his hands till it was as thin as a toothpick. He took another piece and rolled it as thin as a pencil, and pinched one end of each of the two together to make a straight line. He rolled another piece just a bit thicker, and pinched one end of it to the end of the second piece. To keep it in a straight line, he had to move Vinnie's paper.

"Quit that, Charley!" scolded Vinnie.

Charley rolled another piece of clay, a little thicker still. To pinch the end of it to the third piece, he had to move Carl's paper.

"Mr. Sizemore, make Charley quit!" complained Carl.

"What's Charley doing?" asked Mr. Sizemore as he walked over to the table.

"He thinks the whole table belongs to him," said Carl and Vinnie.

"What are you making, Charley?" asked Mr. Sizemore.

"A Thing," said Charley as he rolled another piece.

"You come with me," Mr. Sizemore said. "Bring your clay."

Mr. Sizemore led the way to the room where the blocks were kept. The other children went on painting.

"Since the Thing is so long, why don't you work in here by yourself?" asked Mr. Sizemore. "We'll spread a newspaper on the floor, and you can make your Thing on the paper."

"It'll have to be a long newspaper, Mr. Sizemore," Charley told him. "Because this sure is a long Thing I'm making."

Together Mr. Sizemore and Charley spread newspaper on the floor from the middle of the room up to the door. Then Mr. Sizemore went back into the classroom where the other boys and girls were painting.

Alone in the room, Charley looked at the row of jars of clay standing on the shelf. He took down the jar containing the pink clay and went to work, rolling and rolling, each piece a little thicker than the one before, and pinching the ends together.

Soon Charley had used up all the pink clay there was, and the Thing was not finished. He took down the jar of black clay and went to work again, rolling and rolling, each piece thicker than the one before. He used all the black clay there was. Then he took down the jar of yellow clay and began rolling.

The Thing was finally as big around as Charley's

arm. It had reached almost to the door when the bell rang for the end of the school day.

Charley heard the children in the next room putting away their papers. He heard them getting in line in the hall. He heard Miss Amburgey say, "If you're going to meet that three o'clock bus at Elkhorn, Mr. Sizemore, you'll have to leave right away. I'll take care of your group."

Charley heard more talking and more shuffling of feet down the hall. Then everything grew still.

It was the best day he'd had at Little School. Here he was, all alone, with nobody to tell him "Do this" and "Do that." And the Thing was growing longer and thicker. It was now as thick as a baseball bat, its front end yellow, its middle black, its tail pink.

Charley heard footsteps in Mr. Sizemore's room. For a few seconds everything was quiet. Charley listened. Then he heard the footsteps go away down the hall. He heard Mr. Webb's voice. "Charley! Charley Cornett!"

He'd have to hurry, thought Charley to himself. He took one more piece of yellow clay, shaped it broad and flat, and fastened it to the piece as thick as a baseball bat. That was the Thing's head. The Thing's head lay across the doorsill into Mr. Sizemore's classroom.

Charley stood up and looked at the Thing. He laughed as he thought how scared Mr. Sizemore would be when he walked into his room the next morning and saw the Thing looking at him over the doorsill.

The Thing ought to have a tongue, decided Charley. He took from the jar of red clay one tiny piece. He shaped it thin and short and flat, and fastened it to the Thing's head. The tongue curved upward. Charley stood up to admire it.

He heard steps coming along the hall toward Mr. Sizemore's room. He looked around. There stood Miss Amburgey in the doorway.

"Charley," she scolded, "where have you been?"

"Here," said Charley.

"All the time since the bell rang?"

"Yes'm."

"Why didn't you come with the other children?"

"I wasn't with the other children," said Charley. "They were out here and I was in there."

"But you heard the bell, didn't you?"

"Yes'm."

"Don't you know that when the bell rings it says you must come?" asked Miss Amburgey.

"Yes'm."

"Why didn't you come then?"

"I hadn't finished."

"What hadn't you finished?"

"A Thing I was making."

"Whether you've finished or not, when the bell rings you're to put everything away and come at once. You can finish the next day. Do you know the bus left fifteen minutes ago?"

Charley's face grew serious.

"But I wasn't done," he said.

"What were you doing," asked Miss Amburgey, "that you couldn't leave till tomorrow?"

"I told you, Miss Amburgey, I was making a Thing."

"What kind of thing?"

"Miss Amburgey," said Charley, "shut your eyes and I'll take your hand and lead you to see it. But you won't tell Mr. Sizemore, will you?"

"Charley," said Miss Amburgey sternly, "you know very well—"

She stopped and looked down at Charley.

"All right," she said, and she shut her eyes. Charley took her hand and led her to the door of the room where the blocks stayed.

"Open!" said Charley.

Miss Amburgey opened her eyes.

"Charley! What a snake!" she gasped. "It looks like a real one, except, of course, it is an odd color."

"You know what kind of snake it is?" asked Charley. "It's a yellowblackpink snake and it bites. I'm going to leave it here to scare Mr. Sizemore in the morning."

"Well," said Miss Amburgey, "since you've taken such pains to make the Thing, I guess you may leave it. But come along now. Since the bus has left you, I'll have to take you home myself."

Charley followed her out of the schoolhouse and climbed into her jeep beside her.

What a place school was! thought Charley. He had made the Thing to scare Mr. Sizemore and now he was going to go jeeping home along the blacktop.

As Miss Amburgey turned the key and stepped on the gas pedal, Charley braced himself and ordered, "Now, Miss Amburgey, let 'er tear!"

"You really ought to have to walk home," said Miss Amburgey.

Charley was silent.

"I told Mr. Mullins to stop and tell your mother we couldn't find you, but that, as soon as we did, I'd bring you home. If she weren't worried, I'd let you out right here and start you walking."

They drove along in silence for another minute.

"Miss Amburgey," asked Charley, "how can snakes run so fast when they don't have legs?"

"They're made that way," said Miss Amburgey.

"A rope's made that way too," said Charley, "but it can't run."

They drove another minute in silence.

"You want me to name all the snakes I know?" asked Charley.

"Let's hear them," said Miss Amburgey.

"Rattlesnake. Copperhead snake. Black snake. Chicken snake. Blue racer snake. Garter snake. Water moccasin snake."

"There are books in the library that tell all about snakes," Miss Amburgey said. "And all kinds of snakes that you don't know about, like boa constrictors, and king cobras, and sidewinders. I suspect they even tell how a snake can run fast when it hasn't any legs."

"Sure enough, Miss Amburgey? Books tell you that?"

"They do," said Miss Amburgey. "That's what books are written for."

"Is that what books really do?" asked Charley. "Tell you about things?"

"Books tell you almost anything you will ever want to know," said Miss Amburgey. "Some things, of course, you'll have to find out for yourself."

"When do I go to the library again?" asked Charley.

"This is Wednesday," said Miss Amburgey. "You go to the library day after tomorrow. On Friday."

Miss Amburgey stopped the jeep in front of the Cornetts' mailbox. All the Cornetts were waiting anxiously.

"No need asking," said Claude as Charley climbed out. "You didn't carry the flag today, Charley."

"No," said Charley. "But I made a Thing. Boy, you ought to see it!"

5

The next Monday morning when the bus rolled up beside the Cornetts' mailbox, Mr. Mullins opened the door and scowled. "That you, Charley?" he asked.

"Yep," said Charley as he climbed into the bus.

"I wasn't sure who was under that hat," said Mr. Mullins. "Whose hat is it?"

"Mine," said Charley.

On Charley's head sat an old hat, battered and sweat-stained, and dingy with coal dust. It was made for a man with a head much bigger than Charley's, and it rested so low on Charley's forehead that he had to hold his chin high to see where he was going.

Charley sat down beside Jerry.

"Where'd you get that hat, Charley?" Jerry asked.

"It was give to me."

"Who gave it to you?"

Charley looked straight ahead and said nothing.

Jerry snatched at the hat. Just in time Charley gripped the brim with both hands and held the hat on his head.

Peter tried snatching the hat from behind, then Joey tried snatching it, and Vinnie.

"You, back there!" called Mr. Mullins sternly as he looked into his mirror. "Sit down and leave Charley's hat alone."

When the bus arrived at school, Charley loitered behind as the other boys and girls hurried to the playground. For a minute he stood at the gate looking longingly at them playing leapfrog, going down

the slide, and playing ball with Mr. Webb. Keeping close to the playground fence, he walked down to the creek and stood listening to the water gurgle over the rocks.

When the bell rang, Charley waited until all the other children had passed through the gate. He followed them and stood close beside Miss Amburgey. Inside the classroom, he moved his chair till it was touching Miss Amburgey's, and sat down.

When all the children were seated and had grown quiet, Miss Amburgey said, "Let's talk about something that happened to us after we left school yesterday—something we did, something we saw, something we heard. But," she added, looking down at Charley, "boys don't wear hats inside the room."

Charley sat stiffly and looked at the floor.

"Suppose you hang your hat on that nail by the window, Charley," suggested Miss Amburgey.

Nothing happened.

"Charley!"

Charley turned, tilted his head backward, and looked at Miss Amburgey. "I can't," he said.

"Why not?"

Charley did not answer. He did not move.

"Why not, Charley?"

"I have to keep it on," muttered Charley, looking at the floor. "All day."

"Why?"

"Because."

"All right," said Miss Amburgey, "will you tell us something that happened to you since yesterday? Maybe you can tell us where you got your hat."

Charley said nothing.

"What did happen to you since yesterday, Charley?" asked Miss Amburgey.

"I saw a rabbit," muttered Charley.

"Tell us about the rabbit."

"It was a different rabbit," said Charley.

"How do you know it was different?"

"It hopped different."

"Charley," said Miss Amburgey, "you may wear your hat this morning since for some reason you can't take it off. But if you wear it tomorrow you must take it off when you come in the schoolroom. Do you understand now?"

"Yes'm," said Charley.

Mr. Webb was waiting for the boys and girls

when they came out of Miss Amburgey's room.

"It's such a fine morning," he said, "suppose we walk across the pasture to the woods."

Next to making snakes out of clay, Charley liked best walking to the woods with Mr. Webb. The walk had no sooner started, however, before somebody snatched at Charley's hat. Charley gripped the brim tight with both hands and fell behind the other boys and girls.

"Come on, Charley," called Mr. Webb. He waited until Charley caught up with him.

"Charley," he asked, "where did you get your hat?"

"It was give to me," said Charley. "It's a special kind of hat."

"Is that so!" said Mr. Webb. "Well, maybe you'd better walk beside me."

With one hand Charley held his hat on his head. With the other he held Mr. Webb's hand.

"Look all around you, children," suggested Mr. Webb. "Who can find something interesting?"

As Charley turned to look, somebody snatched at his hat. He almost lost it that time. He grabbed it with both hands and pulled it so far down over

his head that he could see nothing except the ground around him.

"I see something!" shouted Tony. "Up in the sky."

Charley tried to look but he couldn't bend his neck far enough back to see even as high as the tree-tops.

"I see it!" shouted Vinnie. "It's the moon. Coming up right over Mr. Champion's office."

"It's going down, Vinnie," explained Mr. Webb. "It's been up most of the night."

They came to a bridge across a stream that flowed through the pasture.

"Remember the rule about looking into the creek," Mr. Webb reminded them.

The rule was that no one might stand on the edge of the bridge to look into the creek. He had to sprawl flat on the bridge with his head over the edge.

While the others sprawled, Charley stood in the middle of the bridge, holding his hat on his head.

"Charley," asked Mr. Webb, "aren't you going to look? You nearly always find something. I'll hold your hat for you while you look."

"I can't take it off," said Charley.

Charley wished he could look over the edge of the bridge. He knew where minnows had built a nest of fine gravel at the edge of a bed of watercress. He knew where a crawdad hole was. And once he had seen a water snake wriggling up the creek. But if somebody snatched his hat off his head . . .

"Ready to go?" asked Mr. Webb.

The children got up from the bridge. On they went to the woods.

"I see something!" cried Jerry. "Up in that black gum tree. See? One red leaf and all the others are green."

Charley tried to find the leaf, but he couldn't bend his neck far enough back.

"I see a butterfly in the pasture," said Alice.

"Catch it and bring it to me," said Mr. Webb. "I want to show you something."

Alice tiptoed to the knotweed where the butterfly was sipping nectar. She crept up behind it and caught it by both wings. Mr. Webb took it from her gently.

"Can everybody see?" he asked.

They crowded close to him. Charley stood on the edge of the crowd.

"I want to show you this butterfly's tongue," said Mr. Webb.

He put the sharp point of a pencil inside the tight black coil that was the butterfly's tongue and slowly unrolled it.

"Wow!" said Carl as the tongue unrolled longer and longer.

"Can we keep him, Mr. Webb?" asked Vinnie.

"Don't you think he'd rather be free?" asked Mr. Webb. "Suppose I turn him loose and we watch how he flies."

Mr. Webb let go of the butterfly's wings. Quickly the butterfly flew away, up and up and up. The children ran after it.

At the edge of the pasture they stopped and watched the butterfly sail out of sight over the tree-tops.

"Goodbye! Goodbye, butterfly!" the children called.

They waved to him. Charley, holding his hat tight with both hands, waved one finger.

On they went. Hollis was in front. Suddenly he stopped and scooped something up in his hands.

"Look, Mr. Webb!" he called as he came running

with his hands cupped tightly. "Look what I found in the grass."

He opened his hands a crack. Inside sat a tiny toad.

"Put him in my hands," said Danny.

"No, he's mine," said Hollis. "I'll let you feel the bumps on his back."

Around the circle of children went Hollis, letting each one feel the bumps on the toad's back—all but Charley. He longed to feel the toad's bumps, but he was afraid to let go of his hat.

They walked down by the creek. "Look what's here!" called Sam.

He picked up a snake skin from a rock and ran his fingers the length of it.

"Listen!" he said. He ran his fingers the length of it again. "It crackles. Like when the mountain catches on fire."

The boys and girls one by one ran their fingers the length of the snake skin to hear it crackle like fire—all but Charley. At that moment Charley almost wished he didn't have the hat. He longed to feel the snake's skin and to hear it crackle. But as long as he wore the hat, he had to hold on to it to keep some busybody from snatching it off his head.

Mr. Webb looked at his watch.

"It's time now to go to Mr. Sizemore's room," he said.

Mr. Sizemore scowled as Charley walked into the room, holding his hat on his head with both hands.

"You can hang your hat over there by the door, Charley," he said.

Charley looked up at him. He shook his head.

"We always take off our hats in the schoolroom, Charley," said Mr. Sizemore.

"This—this kind of hat you can't take off," explained Charley.

"Is there some reason why you have to wear it?" asked Mr. Sizemore.

Charley nodded his head up and down. "Yes, sir," he said.

"All right," said Mr. Sizemore. "I'll take your word for it."

Of course Charley couldn't make anything out of clay for having to hold on to his hat. He couldn't build with blocks. He couldn't paint. He couldn't color with crayons. It would be mighty handy to have two sets of hands, he thought.

When the bell rang for lunch, the children hurried to get into the line at the cafeteria to have their plates served. Charley, with his hat still on his head, stood at the end of the line.

When Charley's plate was served, he took it and started toward a table in the far corner of the room where no one was sitting.

"Charley Cornett!" he heard someone call.

Charley stopped. He knew the voice. It belonged to Mr. Champion. Charley remembered what John had told him. "When Mr. Champion calls, you better say 'Yes, Sir,' and say it polite like, and get a move on—in Mr. Champion's direction."

Timidly Charley looked in the direction from which the voice had come. There at a table sat Mr. Champion, three girls, and three boys. Beside Mr. Champion was an empty chair.

"Come sit by me, Charley," Mr. Champion invited as he pulled out the chair.

"Yes, Sir," said Charley faintly.

Charley gulped and, with his head down, carried his plate to the table and edged into the chair.

"We men don't usually wear our hats when we eat, Charley," said Mr. Champion. "Why are you wearing yours?"

Charley sat staring at his plate, saying nothing, eating nothing.

"Can you tell me why you're wearing it?" Mr. Champion asked.

Charley shook his head, no.

"Where did you get your hat, Charley?" asked Mr. Champion.

"Uncle Hawk give it to me," said Charley.

"Is your Uncle Hawk at your house now?"

Charley nodded his head, yes.

"He isn't working over at the Benham mines?" asked Mr. Champion.

"He got laid off," Charley told him.

"And he's come to live with your family?"

Charley nodded his head, yes. "Till the mines open again," he said. "He's been mighty nigh everywhere looking for work. But nobody wanted a man to work."

"I see," said Mr. Champion. "And so he gave his hat to you?"

"He slung it on the bed and I picked it up and put it on my head, and Uncle Hawk said, 'I believe I'll give you that hat, boy. I reckon I don't need it any more.' But Mr. Champion, I got to keep it on my head all day. For a special reason."

"It isn't quite the kind of hat boys wear to school, is it?" asked Mr. Champion.

"No," said Charley. "It's a special kind of hat and I got to keep it on my head all day long."

Mr. Champion ate for a minute in silence.

"Tell you what, Charley," he said. "If I were you I'd put that hat away when you get home this afternoon, and save it for special days, like Sundays and the Fourth of July. How about that?"

"That's just what I aim to do," said Charley.

When Charley got off the bus that afternoon, Claude called, "Hey, Charley! Did you carry the flag today?"

"No, I didn't carry the flag today," said Charley. "I didn't do anything today. The hat didn't do anything either," he added.

"What was the hat supposed to do?" asked Connie.

"It's my hat, and what it was supposed to do is my business," said Charley.

He walked straight into the kitchen, took the hat off his head, and hung it on a nail behind the kitchen stove.

6

The next morning as Charley got off the bus, he saw Miss Sturgill talking with Miss Amburgey at the playground gate.

"I don't know how I'm going to finish everything before Friday when school closes," Charley heard Miss Sturgill saying as he went through the gate to the playground. "I have three new cartons of books to catalog, and I certainly could use some help."

Charley turned back. "I can help you, Miss Sturgill," he offered.

"Well," said Miss Sturgill, "that's very good of you, Charley. But I need somebody grown up. Somebody big and strong like Mr. Mullins. Mr. Mullins has built a new bookshelf for the library, and I want to move some books onto it."

"I can move books," said Charley.

Miss Sturgill laid a finger on her cheek and frowned down at Charley. "I suppose you could move books, Charley," she said, "but, if you could read and knew your numbers, you could help me much more."

Charley stood waiting.

Miss Sturgill hesitated. "You really want to help, do you?" she said.

"Yes'm, I do."

"How about it, Miss Amburgey?" asked Miss Sturgill. "Might he be excused from classes today?"

"Certainly," agreed Miss Amburgey. "Helping in the library will be a good way to spend the day. But you must come out to play at recess time, Charley. Right?"

"All right," agreed Charley.

"Well," said Miss Sturgill, "we might as well go along and get busy, Charley."

They started up the stone path to the library, Charley following close behind Miss Sturgill.

"Do you have to know how to read to get a job, Miss Sturgill?" he asked. "Uncle Hawk went mighty nigh ever' place looking for work, but he can't read, and he says it's people that can read get all the jobs."

"Do you know why your Uncle Hawk can't read, Charley?" asked Miss Sturgill. "He never went to school when he was a little boy like you. You see, he lived at the head of Coldiron Branch and the nearest school was nine miles away. He had no bus to take him. He would have had to walk, and a good part of the road ran down the bed of the branch. In winter, during school months, the branch was roaring with water. He could hardly swim to school, could he?"

Charley laughed. "He'd be as wet as I was that day I was a rock, I reckon. But my daddy can read."

"Because your mother taught him," said Miss Sturgill.

They entered the library.

81

"Miss Sturgill," said Charley, "what you want me to do first?"

"Come with me," said Miss Sturgill. She led the way to the shelf in the corner.

"You see, Charley," she explained, "every book has its name and a number on the back of it. That tells us what the book is about."

Charley grinned sheepishly. "Is that why all the books stand on the shelves with their backs turned toward you?" he asked.

"So you're the one who turned a shelf full of them around one day!" said Miss Sturgill. "You see, if a book doesn't stand on the shelf with its back to you, you won't know what it's about. I want you to move all the books from this shelf and put them on the new shelf in exactly the order they are shelved now. Exactly, Charley. Can you do that?"

"I think I can, Miss Sturgill," Charley said.

"I'm going in my office to print numbers on the backs of the new books. When I've finished, I'll help you out here. Shall we get to work now?"

"Sure," said Charley.

At the doorway to her office Miss Sturgill turned. "Let me tell you some things about working,

Charley," she said. "You must always be honest in your work. Whatever you are given to do, you must do just as well when nobody is watching as you would if somebody were standing over you. That's what I mean by being honest in your work."

"Yes'm," said Charley. "I will."

"If you are honest, Charley, and if you are useful, you are a valuable person. And if you know a great deal about something—oh, about almost anything— you'll find work in some place."

"Yes'm," said Charley. "You know what I want to know everything about?"

"What?" asked Miss Sturgill.

"Snakes."

"Snakes!" Miss Sturgill's voice rose to a high pitch. "All right. Let's get to work."

Miss Sturgill disappeared into her office.

A minute later Charley called, "Miss Sturgill, this new shelf is too dusty to put books on. You want me to dust it?"

"I thought it was dusted yesterday, Charley," she answered. "But if you think it isn't clean, you may dust it again. You'll find the dust cloth in the closet in the hall."

Charley found the dust cloth and set to dusting. In a few minutes he called, "Miss Sturgill, am I being useful?"

"Very useful."

Charley dusted some more.

"Miss Sturgill," he called, "am I being honest?"

"I'll come and see," said Miss Sturgill. She got up from her office desk and went into the library.

"Charley, you're being very honest indeed," she said. "I believe you can start moving the books now."

She went back into her office.

After a while Charley called again.

"Miss Sturgill, do you know why I wore my hat all day yesterday?"

Miss Sturgill got up from her desk, walked into the library, and stood beside Charley.

"We've all wondered why you wore it, Charley," she said.

"Well," said Charley, "I'll tell you. When Uncle Hawk was looking for work, he went to a lot of great big cities. And he told us all the sights he saw —houses so high you couldn't hardly see the tops of 'em, and streets as wide as a cow pasture. And them cities, he says, are all so lit up at night, anybody wouldn't know if it was daytime or nighttime."

"Yes, Charley," said Miss Sturgill, "cities are like that."

"When Uncle Hawk give me his hat, first thing I thought of was that story you told us about the man that flew all over on a magic carpet. You know that story?"

"Yes," said Miss Sturgill.

"Well, I made out like Uncle Hawk's hat was magic, too. And if I wore it all day and didn't once take it off my head—"

"Or let anybody snatch it off," said Miss Sturgill.

Charley laughed. "Or let anybody snatch it off," he said, "it'd be magic like the old man's carpet, and it'd pick me up and take me sailing off to see all them sights Uncle Hawk saw."

"I see, Charley," said Miss Sturgill.

She stood for a minute looking at him.

"I'm sorry the hat disappointed you," she said thoughtfully. "But you can work another kind of magic, and someday, not now but when you're older, I think you can go flying off to see even more wonderful sights than Uncle Hawk saw."

"How, Miss Sturgill?"

"If you are an honest boy and do honest and useful work, and if you learn everything you can about something—say about spaceships—"

"Snakes," Charley corrected her.

"Oh, I forgot. Snakes," said Miss Sturgill. "Let's say you learn everything you possibly can learn about snakes. Look here."

She turned to the wall behind them on which hung a large map of the world, and pointed to one spot on the map.

"Here in a country named Brazil," she said, "is a city where there is a famous snake farm."

"A snake farm?"

"Yes. They keep poisonous snakes there. And they take the poison from the snakes and make it into medicine to cure people who have been bitten by poisonous snakes."

"Wow!" said Charley.

"Suppose," said Miss Sturgill, "one day a letter comes to the President of the United States. It says, 'Dear Mr. President of the United States: Out in the jungle we have caught a snake which is different from any we have ever seen. Will you please send

Mr. Charles Cornett down here to tell us what it is?" She paused a second while Charley stared at her with his mouth open. " 'Postscript,' she added. 'Send him by the fastest jet plane. We will pay for his ticket.' "

"Aw, Miss Sturgill, really?" Charley grinned broadly. "Magic like that? Do you really mean that?"

"Oh," said Miss Sturgill, "that. Or something like that."

"That would be more fun than flying on an old carpet," said Charley.

"Well," said Miss Sturgill, "it's up to you to make it happen. Now let's get back to work."

When the bell rang for recess, Charley put his head in at the office door.

"Do I have to go out and play, Miss Sturgill?" he asked.

"What do you think, Charley?" asked Miss Sturgill.

Charley grinned. "I think yes."

"I think yes, too," said Miss Sturgill. "You must always do what you agree to do."

Out went Charley.

When the bell rang for the end of recess, Miss

Sturgill heard Charley tiptoe into the library. He tiptoed up to her office door and stood with his hands behind him. "I've got something for you," he said.

He brought from behind his back a poplar leaf and on it a handful of small, pale cream-colored rocks.

"Goose rocks!" exclaimed Miss Sturgill. "Aren't they beautiful! I never saw goose rocks sparkle so."

"I washed 'em in the creek," explained Charley. "I hunted them while the others played, and wiped them on my shirt tail and put them on this poplar leaf. I think goose rocks are pretty as dandelions, don't you?"

"I certainly do, Charley," said Miss Sturgill. "I'll enjoy having them here on my desk. And some day we'll find a book about rocks and learn why these are called goose rocks."

"They're called goose rocks because geese eat 'em," said Charley. "Didn't you know that? Geese need 'em in their craws."

"Charley," asked Miss Sturgill, "have you ever had a book of your own?"

Charley shook his head, no.

"We got no books in our house at all," he said.

"If you're going to know everything about snakes," said Miss Sturgill, "you'll have to have books about snakes. Among these new books is one about snakes with lots of pictures in it, and I'm going to give it to you to start your own library. I'll order another one for the school library."

Charley reached for the book, and then drew back his hand.

"The book is yours, Charley, to take home with you and keep. See?" Miss Sturgill opened the book. "I've written your name in it."

Charley hesitated. "Does that make it mine?"

"Yes," said Miss Sturgill.

A wide grin spread slowly across Charley's face. He took the book from Miss Sturgill and hugged it.

Fifteen minutes later Miss Amburgey came by the library. Miss Sturgill called to her, "Can you stop in a minute?"

At first their voices coming from the office were so low that Charley could not understand what they said as he moved books from the old shelf to the new one.

After a minute he heard Miss Amburgey say, "I'm going to drive over the mountain to Elkhorn after

school this afternoon. Any errands I can do for you?"

"No, I believe not," said Miss Sturgill. "Maybe I'll ride along with you as far as Charley's house and tell his mother what a good job Charley's done today. You can pick me up on the way home."

When the bell rang at the end of the schoolday, all the children gathered together at the schoolhouse door.

"Let me carry the flag, Miss Amburgey."

A dozen boys and girls were asking to carry the flag.

"Get in line, children," said Miss Amburgey.

They formed a long line. Charley stood at the end of the line, hugging his book tightly.

"Charley," said Miss Amburgey, "you may carry the flag today."

"Charley!" the children shouted in surprise.

Charley looked at Miss Amburgey, but he didn't move. He stood very still, hugging his book.

"Charley, don't you want to carry the flag?" asked Miss Amburgey.

Charley shook his head, no.

"Everybody wants to carry the flag, Charley,"

said Miss Amburgey. "And Miss Sturgill said you had been very helpful in the library."

Still Charley stood at the back of the line.

"Why don't you want to carry the flag, Charley?" Miss Amburgey asked.

"Somebody might snatch my book," Charley explained.

"Oh, no," said Miss Amburgey. "Nobody's going to snatch your book."

She walked to the foot of the line where Charley stood.

"Hold your book under one arm, like this," she said, tucking the book under his left arm. "And hold the flag high with your other hand," she said, placing the flag in his right hand. "Move along now to the head of the line. The bus is waiting."

With a proud grin on his face, Charley walked to the head of the line. In his right hand he held the flag high, and with his left arm he tightly hugged his book.

When the bus stopped at the Cornett mailbox, Charley tumbled out and started in a run down the steep path to the house, shouting, "Mom! Mom! Uncle Hawk!"

All the Cornetts came hurrying. Uncle Hawk came too.

Charley threw his arms about his mother's waist.

"Why, Charley," said Mrs. Cornett, "I believe you carried the flag today."

"Look, Mom, what I've got!" said Charley. "Look, Uncle Hawk. Miss Sturgill give me this book. It's all about snakes. She wrote my name in it. That says it's mine. To keep."

He opened the book and showed them his name.

"Charley Cornett. His first book about snakes. From Miss Sturgill," read Mrs. Cornett.

"See? That means it's mine," said Charley. "And I'm going to have a library as big as Miss Sturgill's library at school. And every book in it is going to be about snakes. Uncle Hawk, it—it's sort of like magic."

"That so?" said Uncle Hawk.

"Well," said Connie, "what about the flag, Charley?"

"Oh," said Charley, "yes. I carried the flag today, too."

"Charley, I'm proud of you!" his mother said. She put her arms around him.

"Hooray for Charley!" shouted Claude.

All the other Cornetts clapped their hands.

Just at that moment Miss Sturgill and Miss Amburgey drove up in the jeep. When Mrs. Cornett heard their plans, she said, "Now we've got to celebrate for Charley. Claude brought a big ripe watermelon from the patch and it's in the creek cooling. When you come back, Miss Amburgey, we'll have a watermelon cutting in Charley's honor."

"Fine," said Miss Amburgey. "Charley," she asked, "how would you like to ride over to Elkhorn with me?"

"You can go, Charley," said Mrs. Cornett. "It's mighty nice to have such good things happening to you all at once."

With a grin on his face, Charley climbed into the jeep and slammed the door shut. Miss Amburgey climbed in on the other side, slammed her door, turned the key, and put her foot on the gas pedal. Charley braced himself.

"Now, Miss Amburgey," he said, "let 'er tear."

"All right," said Miss Amburgey. "I will."